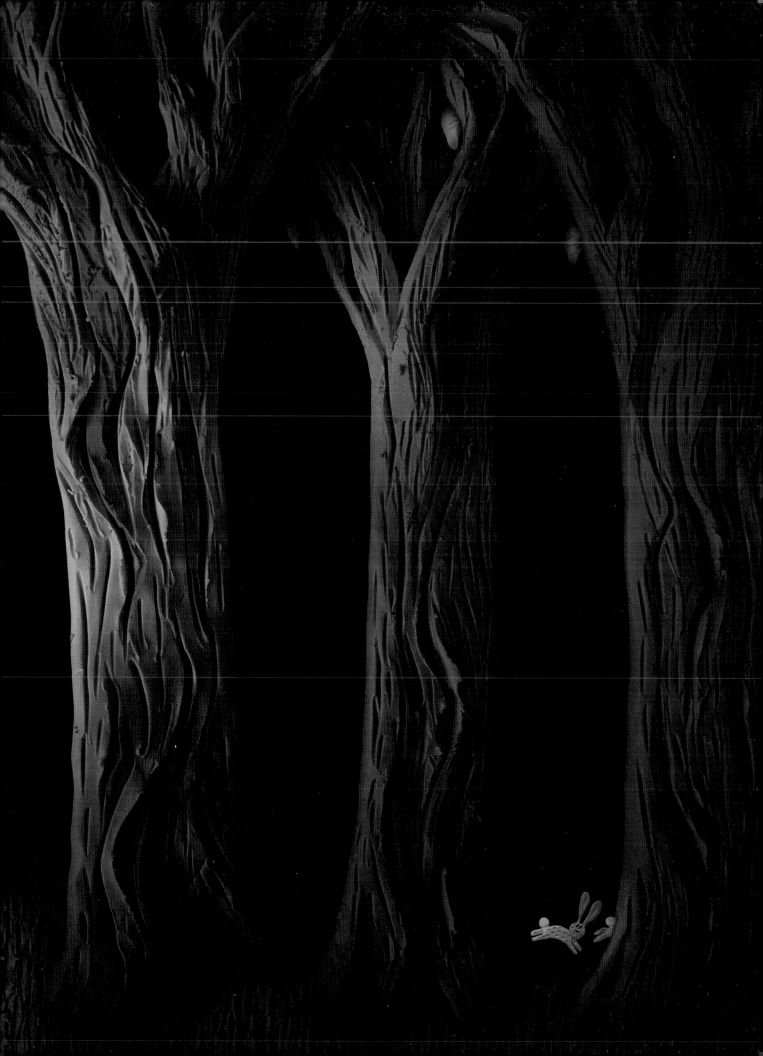

For my family,
Kelly, Benjamin, and Edward.

And for my high school art teacher,
Mrs. Elam.

• A NOTE ON THE ART •

Each piece of art begins with a rough pencil sketch projected onto a piece of glass as a guide for sculpting. The illustration is shaped in clay by hand, then wooden tools are used to create the smallest details. The clay sculptures are photographed outdoors in natural light and then digitally painted with as little retouching as possible. I can say my fingerprints are literally all over this book!

Although the worlds in this book live in my head, when I sculpt them in clay they become real. I can touch them, light them, and look at them from different angles. Each clay sculpture takes its own time to create. Whether I am sculpting the trees or clouds or characters, I feel like I am truly immersed in this little world. It's real to me. I just love it.

BLOOMSBURY CHILDREN'S BOOKS
Bloomsbury Publishing Plc
50 Bedford Square, London WC1B 3DP, UK

BLOOMSBURY, BLOOMSBURY CHILDREN'S BOOKS and the Diana logo are trademarks of Bloomsbury Publishing Plc

First published in the USA 2021 by Bloomsbury Children's Books
1385 Broadway, New York, New York 10018
This edition published in Great Britain in 2021 by Bloomsbury Publishing Plc

Text and Illustrations copyright © Andy Harkness, 2021

Andy Harkness has asserted his right under the Copyright, Designs and Patents Act, 1988,
to be identified as Author and Illustrator of this work

A catalogue record for this book is available from the British Library

ISBN 978 1 5266 2249 5 (HB)
ISBN 978 1 5266 2250 1 (PB)
ISBN 978 1 5266 2248 8 (eBook)

2 4 6 8 10 9 7 5 3 1

Printed in China by Leo Paper Products, Heshan, Guangdong

All papers used by Bloomsbury Publishing Plc are natural, recyclable products from wood grown in well-managed forests.
The manufacturing processes conform to the environmental regulations of the country of origin

To find out more about our authors and books visit www.bloomsbury.com and sign up for our newsletters

# WOLFBOY

ANDY HARKNESS

BLOOMSBURY
CHILDREN'S BOOKS
LONDON  NEW YORK  OXFORD  NEW DELHI  SYDNEY

The moon was full.

Wolfboy stomped beneath the shadowy trees.
He was **HUNGRY**.

"Rabbits, rabbits! Where are you?" he howled.
But the rabbits were nowhere to be found.

Wolfboy sploshed across the murky creek.
He was **HUNGRY**
and **HUFFY**.

"Rabbits, rabbits! Where are you?"

Wolfboy climbed up the creaky old oak.

He was **HUNGRY**
and **HUFFY**
and **DROOLY**.

He needed rabbits.

"Rabbits, rabbits! Where are you?"

Wolfboy slogged through the soggy bog.

He was **HUNGRY**
and **HUFFY**
and **DROOLY**
and **GROWLY**.

"Rabbits, rabbits!
Where are you?"

Wolfboy leaped across

the steep ravine . . .

. . . and marched into Moonberry Meadow.

He was **HUNGRY**
and **HUFFY**
and **DROOLY**
and **GROWLY**
and **FUSSY**.

"Rabbits, rabbits! Where are you?" he howled.
But the rabbits were nowhere to be found.

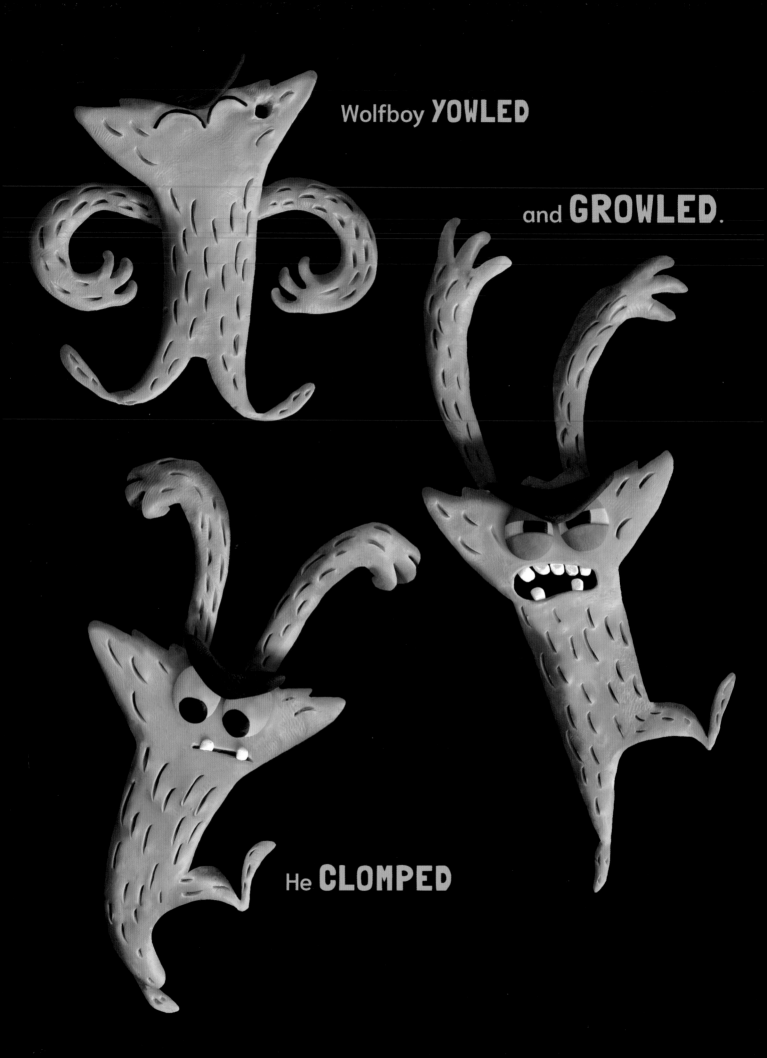

and **TROMPED**.

**"I NEED FOOD!"**

he roared.

Suddenly, there was a rustle of grass.

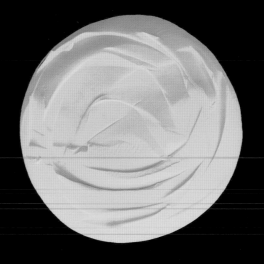

Wolfboy froze.

A twig snapped.

Wolfboy's eyes sharpened.

Then he saw two long ears . . .

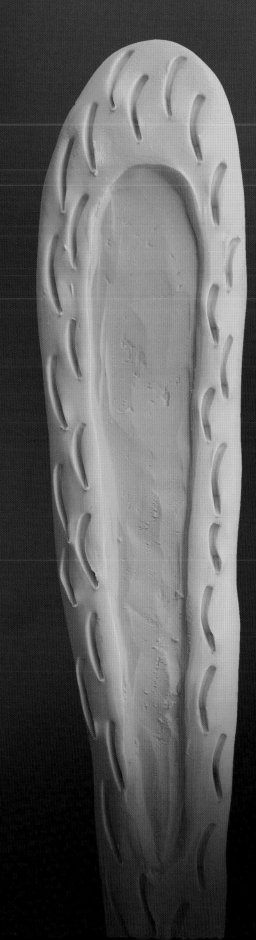
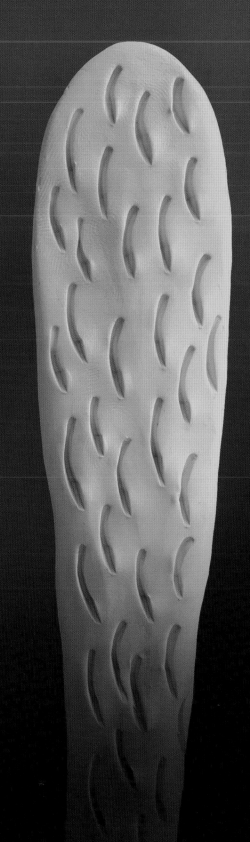

A furry foot.

And a cottony tail.

His tummy rumbled loudly.

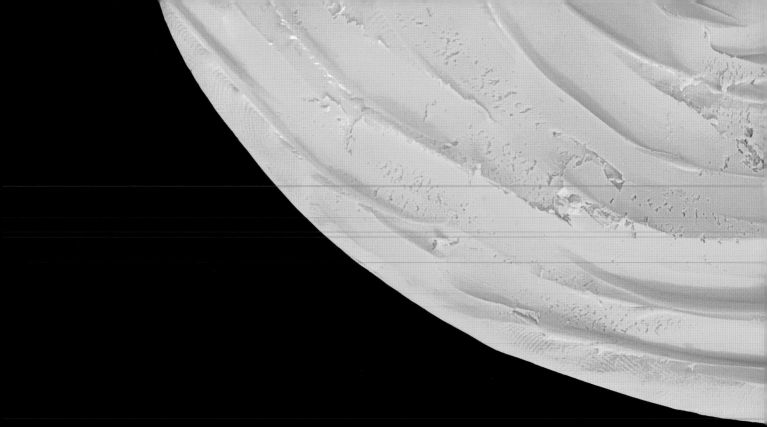

Wolfboy
crouched
low.

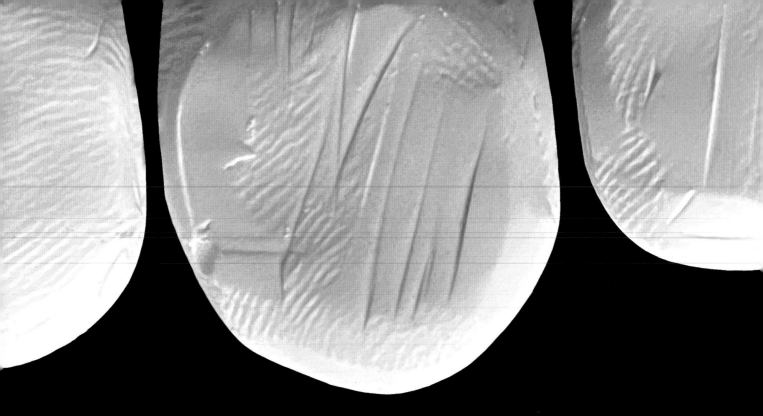

One by one, little rabbits hopped
out of the shadows.

Wolfboy opened his big
**SNARLING** snout . . .

and licked his lips hungrily.

He was **DROOLY**
and **GROWLY**
and **FUSSY**.

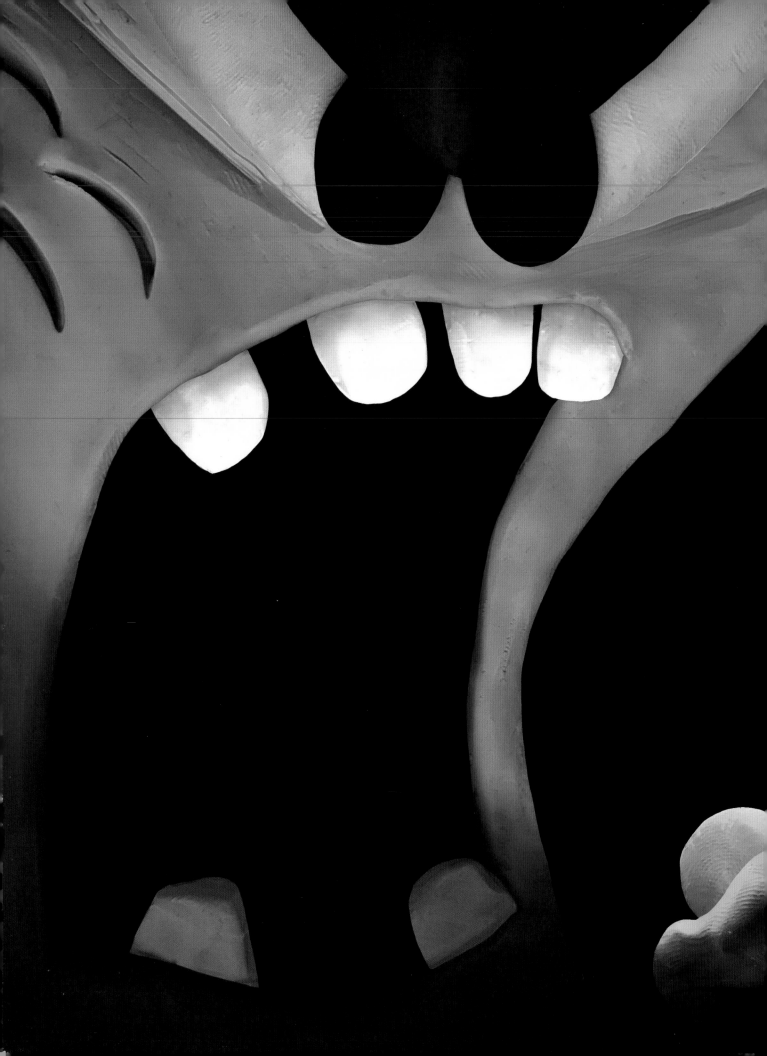

"Rabbits, where have you been?
You're late for our feast!"

"Oh Wolfboy," the rabbits said playfully,
"we made you a moonberry pie!"

Wolfboy gulped. Then he . . .

...CRUNCHED
and MUNCHED
and GOBBLED
and GULPED!

"Rabbits, I was just so **HUNGRY**
and **HUFFY**
and **DROOLY**
and **GROWLY**
and **FUSSY**."

"And don't forget **HOWLY!**"
the rabbits said.

"But now I am . . .

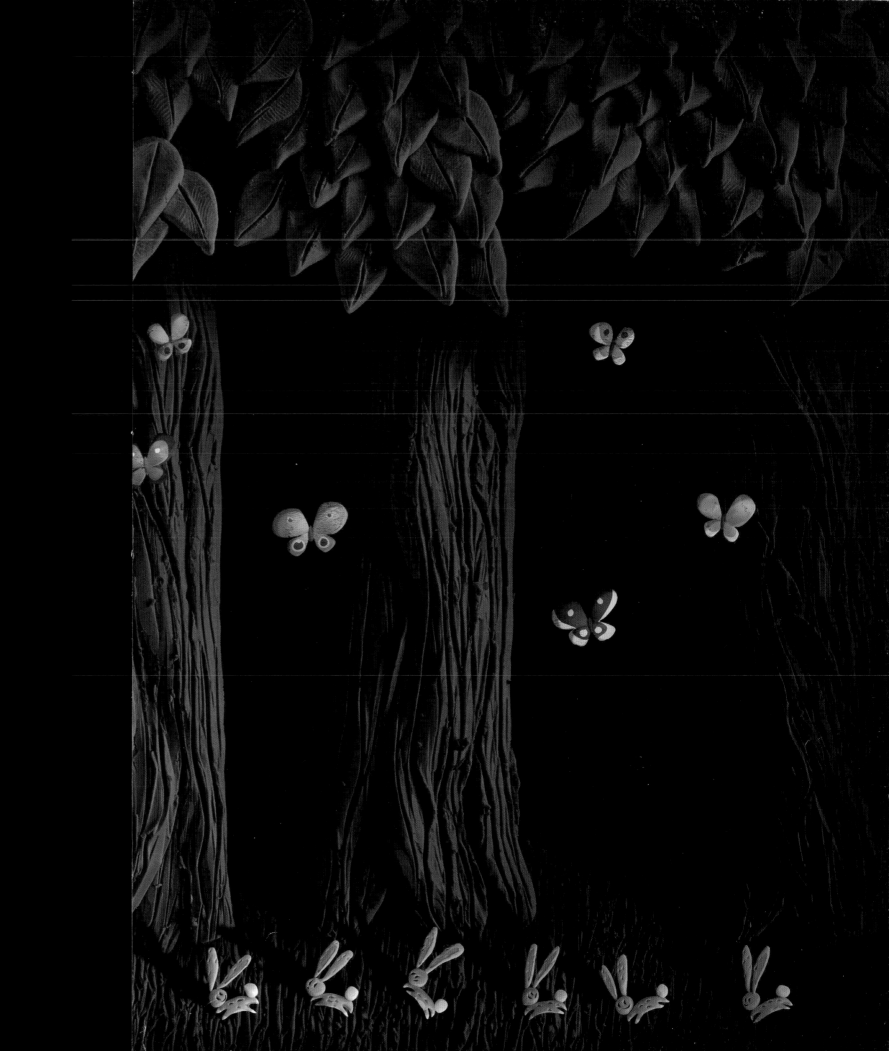

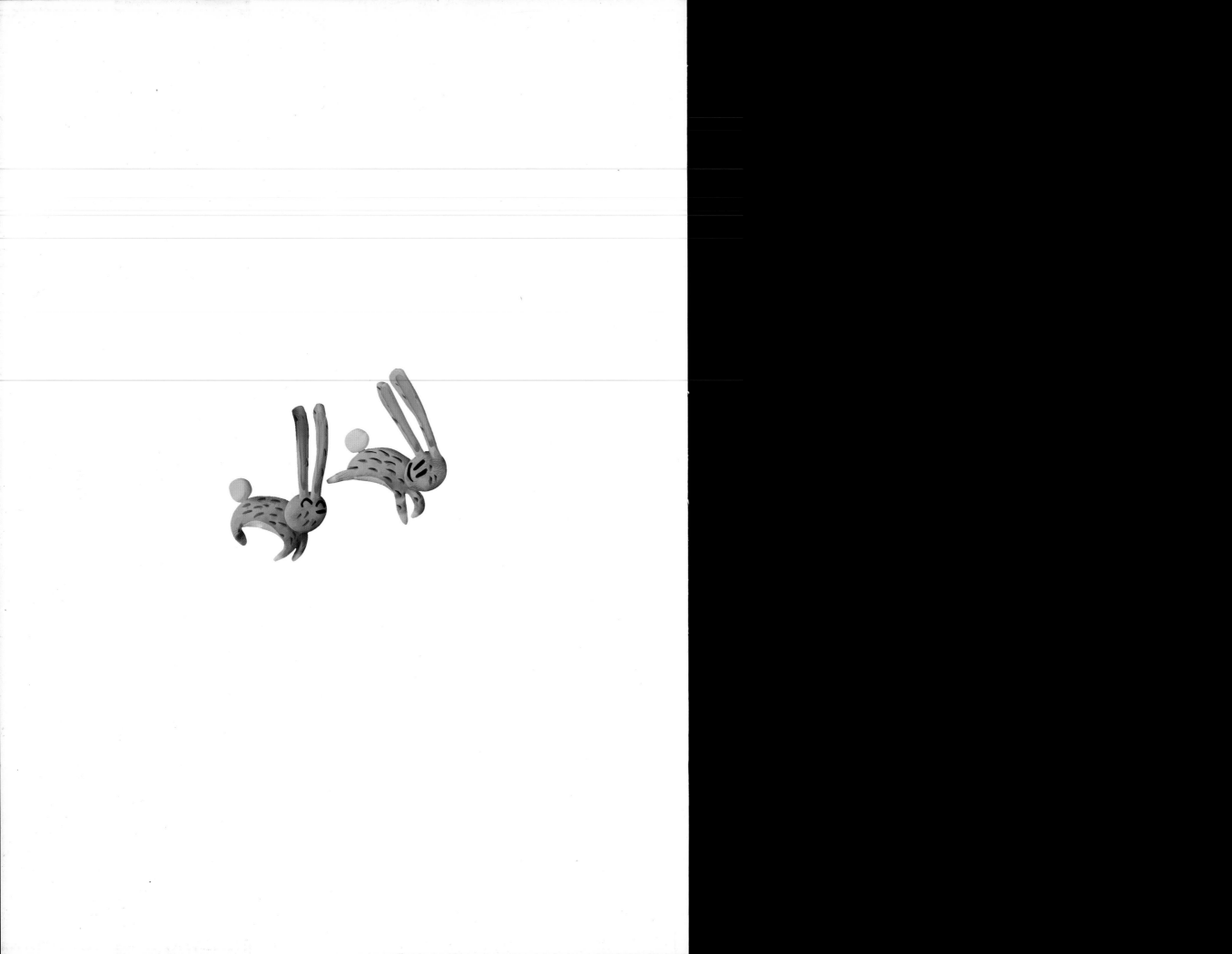